BATTLEGROUND

An Undead Prequel

By

J.E. Taylor

Battleground © 2020 J.E. Taylor

Cover Art by julienicholls.com

BATTLEGROUND

Dumb luck saved my ass more than once, but it won't save me now.

The day the world as we knew it ended, I was dealing with a broken-down car in the sweltering heat.

One choice saved my life.

One single action prevented whatever turned the world into flesh-eating fiends from turning me alongside them.

And now, I'm on the run, desperate to survive.

All I need is to find someone else who lived through that initial damnation.

Someone like me.

Chapter 1

MY HEART DRUMS so hard, it pulses in my throat. The bodies shuffle outside the reinforced plexiglass restlessly. It's as if they can smell me through the concrete fortress encasing me. I close my eyes and grip my weapons tightly, praying they go by, but I know that is just wishful thinking.

I take shallow breaths, trying to minimize the disruption of air around me. And I count silently in my head, guessing at the number of dead surrounding my little hiding spot. It might as well be a grave, what with my chances of surviving an onslaught.

I nearly laugh out loud. Based on my original level of survival skills, I should have been one of the dead a long time ago, but dumb luck saved my ass time and time again. I wonder when my lucky streak will end.

The thought sends a shiver up my spine and my body jerks in response.

Movement outside ceases and sniffing sounds fill the space.

I try to make myself smaller, to hold my breath, to calm my heart so I stop sweating. I need to stop sweating. That's a sure tell that a breathing body is inhabiting the fort.

In an effort to calm myself, I squeeze my eyes tighter and let my mind drift back to the beginning. Or the end, whichever seems more appropriate. I smile at my internal monologue and then force my thoughts to the day the world turned to shit.

The day dumb luck became my welcomed friend.

THE ALARM HAD gone off for the third time that morning. I slammed the snooze once more before a single eye opened to see what time it actually was. Ugh. I was already later than normal, so I dragged my ass out of bed, mumbling under my breath at the fact I had to work another long shift as a cube grunt. It could be worse; I could be out baking in the sun all day instead of being in an air-conditioned eight-by-eight cube, staring at a computer and trying to be helpful to the ungrateful callers.

Customer service was its own kind of hell, but in retrospect, I didn't know just how good I had it.

Halfway to the office, my car blew a tire, and I had to pull over in the breakdown lane. I leaned back in the seat and wiped my face, aggravated that I would be written up this time for not making the start of my shift. I climbed out of the car into the sweltering summer heat. The kind of heat that steals your breath the minute you step out into it and turns your skin tacky on contact. Muttering, I opened the hatchback and pushed the towels and crumpled fast-food bags out of the way to get to the spare tire well. When I lifted the carpet floor, I stared at the empty wheel well. The standard jack wasn't even in the compartment. I slammed the trunk closed and leaned on it, watching the skyscrapers poking out over the horizon of the hill looming before me. Drivers zoomed by without giving me a second look.

The last straw was the single bar of service and the low power on my phone. I slid into the car, looking for my charger, which was inconveniently still at home. My phone had just enough juice for me to get a call into a tow service but then it died.

It wasn't until my car sputtered that I believed I had been blasted with some kind of curse this particular morning. My nice, cool, air-conditioned waiting room had also run out of gas.

I didn't have enough time to even crack a window.

Dead car. Dead phone. Just my luck. I stepped out of the car and promptly broke a heel on my shoes. I stood, looking at my mangled sandal, and caught the gym bag in my backseat out of the corner of my eye. I would roast in the nylons and women's knit suit I had on. I glanced at the woods at the edge of the grassy knoll. There was enough cover to change out of the dress I was wearing and into my comfy workout clothes.

With my gym bag and pocketbook clutched in my hand, I limped across the grass and stepped into the woods to find a tree big enough to block me from view. Although I thought that had to be one of the worst days of my life, it turned out to be another case of blind luck.

As soon as I finished tying my shoe and was reaching for the heap of already sweaty clothing on the ground, the first squeal of tires reached my ears. It was followed by the distinct sound of a crash. But it wasn't just one crunch: it was a whole cacophony of twisted metal.

The ground rumbled beneath me and the trees bowed in the wind, as if they were protecting me in a green shield against whatever had happened outside my little cocoon.

It took awhile for the ground to stop shaking. And it took me even longer to untangle myself from the greenery. The highway was a mass of mangled vehicles. And yet no one screamed. No one cried for help. No sirens wailed in the distance. Only deathly silence blanketed the accident scene.

I glanced toward the city and froze. A gray mushroom cloud loomed over what used to be the city. The buildings looked similar to the cars in front of me—twisted metal blowing smoke.

The woods shielded me from whatever weapon was unleashed that day.

Chapter 2

THE WINDOW ABOVE me rattles and I push farther into the alcove underneath it so dead eyes can't see me.

I had had so little time to prepare myself for the devastation that day because it wasn't long after the silence settled that the dead began to rise. Fortunately for me, their growling grunts were confined to the car interiors.

However, the few bodies thrown from the cars were the ones that had me running. I had seen enough zombie shows on television to understand. I was enough of a horror geek to turn on my heels and run. Away from the mangled highway, away from the destroyed city.

Dumb luck favored me, because I was able to get away now that I had sneakers on. Finding a suitable hiding place had been rougher, but I stumbled upon this small survival camp that obviously hadn't been used in years. The old metal door had creaked when I opened it and slid inside. However, the locking mechanism on the inside seemed much more secure than I could have ever hoped for. The sparse furnishings of a kitchen table and a couple of broken chairs was enough for me to hide away from the dingy window and the noises beyond.

I just hoped that there were more like me. More who had been spared by a random act of God.

So far, survivors eluded me, and I was losing hope fast, especially after months of these lonely survival runs to whatever houses I could find within running distance of my hideout.

The number of houses I pillaged over the last few months gave me what little I had. My machete and my hellraiser and the few plastic bottles of water was all I had left. There was nothing more out there to plunder.

My hellraiser had been more of a surprise find than anything else. The sum of some weird parts put together into a weapon that had served me well. I had found an old broomstick in one of the garages that I plucked through. Along with a drawer of nails sitting in the middle of the concrete floor, as if forgotten in the flash of death that took the homeowner. But it was the rubber doll head that sat just as abandoned as the drawer of nails that chilled me. I stared at the broomstick for hours, trying to figure out how to make it into a weapon. I didn't have enough grace to handle it as just a staff alone. I needed it to be deadly. But all I had at my disposal were the steel nails, the broomstick, and that rubbery discarded doll head.

At the bottom of the nail drawer sat an unopened instant-glue tube. That glue got me thinking.

I started playing with the doll head, putting it on and off the screw end of the broomstick. I guess being alone and terrified for months really made me a little more off-kilter than normal. And my doll head seemed more and more like a "Wilson" to me, except it would not hold up against the horde in its current condition.

I glanced at the sharp nails in that drawer and another idea surfaced. One that made that discarded doll into my trusty personal Hellraiser.

I stare at the deadly head shaking in my grip and force my breath to even out. My eyes dart around the corners of the room as the small sound of nails on concrete catches my attention. Searching, my gaze lands on a rat, and my mouth waters. It has been awhile since I had anything substantial to eat, but I will have to pass on smashing the rodent's head under my metal club. That would be a sure way to die today.

Its little head jerks up and eyes widen at the window rattling above me. It turns and squeezes through a crack in the wall. It only takes a moment, but all activity outside my window stops. Lumbering footsteps head away from my hiding place and sooner than I anticipate, the squeal of the rat reaches my ears.

The dead are getting faster, smarter, and they've started hunting in packs.

One would think they would decay to dust, but that takes years. I don't have years, and I need my own living pack. I must find other survivors and hiding in this concrete room won't help.

I hold my breath and listen again, but there is no sound outside my fortress. It's as if the zombie horde has moved on. My stomach growls and my gaze moves to the crack the rat ran out of, hoping that somehow another meal would present itself. But I know better. I need to leave this shelter in order to find food, and perhaps this time, I'll find living beings.

I stow my weapons into their holders on my back and move to the iron door. Unlatching it slowly and as silently as the crusted latches allow, I pause to make sure the sound did not reach the zombie horde's ears. When no rustling from outside penetrates the walls, I exhale slowly and try the door. The rusty hinges scream their siren and I almost close the door out of fear it is loud enough to call the flesh eaters back. But the fresh breeze and empty field in front of my hiding place pulls me forth.

I glance back at the stale, dank room and the empty cans strewn across the floor. Evidence of all the meals I had amassed and burned through over the last month, my last of which had to have been a week ago, which was why my stomach was so insistent on food. I grab the last water bottle and shut the door on my latest hideout.

Trepidation fills me and I look both ways, listening to the eerie silence, curtailing my instinct to flee. If the pack is out there waiting, and I run, there will be nowhere to retreat, and I will end up like the rat.

I wipe my palms on my ripped sweatpants, thankful for the sneakers that are nearly falling apart. The alternative had been broken stilettos. And if I had those on the first time I was chased, I'd be one of the undead right now.

I'd have to find sneakers that fit soon. These trusty running shoes were not going to last much longer.

I bolt across the open field, crouching low so I'm nearly swallowed by the grass. The woods seem like miles away, but in reality, it's only a couple hundred yards. The fast-moving trek depletes me of all my energy.

I lean against the tree, ducking my head around the wide bark to make sure nothing lies beyond.

Nothing moves. I let go of a breath I am holding and lower myself to the ground. I uncap my water and take a small sip. Even though I crave more, I cap the bottle and slide it into my pocket to keep both hands free. Although I would love nothing more than fifteen minutes of shut-eye, that's the fastest way to become one of the undead.

So, I force myself up on my feet again and move farther away from my little steel trap. I could have never made it a couple of weeks in that concrete can during the heat of the summer. But with the fall nip in the air, the interior never seemed to go higher than seventy. However, with winter fast approaching, I need to find somewhere to hunker down.

Preferably with an endless supply of canned goods, some warm clothes, and some decent weapons, but I know that is an impossible ask.

But still, a girl can dream, right?

Chapter 3

NIGHTFALL IS THE time terror grips me the most. I cannot see what is coming and that always leaves my heart racing and my mouth like the Sahara. I am not even sure what state I am in, never mind what town, because I shy away from open spaces. I choose to stay in the woods as opposed to lumbering down the streets in the open like a fool.

The shelter of the trees makes me feel safer, although right now, that truth is on shaky ground. I test out each footstep, making sure the forest floor is solid before I put the rest of my weight down. There had been too many times I happened on fresh kills that hadn't reanimated yet, and I wish to avoid that slick awfulness if I can help it.

Light seeps into the woods from the full moon above and my vision seems to clear. But that in itself isn't good. If I can see the trees, the dead can see me. I cling to the nearest tree, listening to the nothingness. Not even a cricket's song penetrates the silence.

A flare of light crosses my path, and I dodge behind the tree. I blink at the ray sweeping the woods and I hold my breath.

"Shush," a voice whispers. "I saw something." The shuffle of leaves underfoot reaches my ears as well.

My brain is slow to register, but when it does, I nearly jump out from behind the tree. Except at the last moment, I hear the cock of a firearm. That keeps me in place. If I jump out now, I'm liable to get shot and die. That wouldn't be so bad, but if the bullet doesn't penetrate my brain, then I will turn into one of those things and I cannot have that.

I reach behind me and slowly pull out my spiked staff as quietly as possible. I don't want to chance a gunshot. But I also do not want to lose the human connection, especially because it has literally been months since I've seen anyone living.

With a deep breath, I take the gamble. "Um, hi," I say, loud enough for whoever has the flashlight to hear, but not loud enough to echo and bring damnation upon us. I wave the staff slowly out in the open, just in case they are as taken aback as I am by another human voice.

All movement stops and the flashlight shines on my waving staff. The end of it glistens in the light, illuminating the deadly spikes coming out of the end like some horrible nightmare version of Hellraiser on a stick. At least it wasn't a human head. But the doll's head version I glued to the staff worked amazingly well against the undead that had gotten close enough for me to play whack-a-mole with.

But as I wave the gore-laden head in and out of the light, I wonder whether it really had been the most practical of weapons, or whether it just screamed crazy.

"Don't shoot." I take a deep breath and peer around the tree. Their light blinds me, and I squint, trying to see the four shadows in more detail. The light drops to the ground and all I'm left with is white spots in my vision.

"Did you make that thing?" one of them asks.

It's a decidedly female voice, but it has enough incredulousness in the tone for me to smile. "Yeah." I step out from behind the tree so they can see I'm not some psycho lunatic. I'm just a thirty-something working woman who got caught with her pants down.

My eyes finally adjust, and I scan four girls in their mid to late teens.

"Where were you when it happened?" I ask as I search each mud-streaked face.

They all look down and then at the one who seems the oldest. The darker-haired girl gives me a half smile. "Partying in the woods." She then glances at my outfit. "Jogging?"

I let out a laugh and look down at the sensible sweatpants

and T-shirt I'm wearing. "No. My car broke down, and I would have wilted if I stayed in my work clothes while I waited for the tow truck. So, I grabbed my gym bag and went into the woods to change." I shrugged. "I think my car breaking down saved me."

The petite, dark girl laughed. "I'm sure it did. Anyone hiding in the woods seems to have been spared."

Hope sparks in my soul. "There are more than just the five of us?"

The older girl eyes me warily. Her gaze keeps going to my makeshift weapon, like I did fall into that crazy zone I had been initially worried about. "We've run into a few."

"Where are they?" I'm almost salivating at the thought of seeing other people.

The girls glance at each other and shrug, dashing my momentary excitement.

"Do you have any food?" The blonde narrows her eyes.

I shake my head. I still haven't found a bite to eat and my water bottle only has a splash or two left. I keep it in case I run into a stream and then I fill it by covering the top with my ribbed shirt to try to filter out the worst of the contaminants.

But I hadn't even found a water supply in my trek today.

"Do you have food?" I lick my lips, hoping they have something, even if it's junk food. I could eat just about anything right now.

"No." The dark-haired girl glances around in that skittish fashion that I recognize.

I've been there more times than not over the last few months. It's the look of paranoia.

"My name's Kate and I'm originally from Connecticut." I

stick out my free hand to no one in particular.

They all stare at my flesh as if it's foreign. And then the redhead steps in and connects her hand to mine, gripping it lightly in a quick shake. "Amber." She then steps back, looking at the other three as if they need to be polite and shake my hand.

The blonde gives her a cross glare and then shakes my hand as if I'm poison. "Sarah." She steps away, waving the other two in.

The petite girl holding a staff that looks like a work of carved art reaches in next. "Kya," she says, and her dark hand nearly disappears in mine as she shakes my hand. But her grip is surer and steadier than the other two.

Which leaves the brunette, who stares at me as though I'm not to be trusted. Yet she does offer her hand, but I need to reach out to clasp my palm to hers. "Carrie." She pulls her hand away just as quickly, wiping it on her pants as if I could be carrying whatever horrifying thing turned humanity into horror movie monsters.

I lick my lips and glance around. "I wouldn't head in that direction." I point the way I had come. "I'm trying to put as much distance between me and the last horde I saw. What about the direction you came?" I nod toward the path they navigated.

Carrie shook her head. "They nearly overwhelmed us."

I look beyond her and then back, thinking about the rat. "How did you get away?"

She points upward. "Trees." And then she shows me the bottom of her shoes. Climber spikes are secured to each shoe. "It's how we've been able to get out of their scent range. I don't think they can see because they never attempted to climb up to where we hid."

That's some good intel. If nothing else develops with these girls, at least I'll have an effective way of avoiding a zombie attack. But I will have to venture out to a sporting goods store to get climbing cleats. I needed other things for the coming winter if I haven't found any sort of civilization by then, too, so my hiatus in the woods will be ending much sooner than I had hoped.

"Do you know where I can get some of those?" I ask, because I have no idea how close or how far I am from civilization.

"There's a mall a few miles back, but it's pretty much overrun with them. But we were able to sneak into the sporting goods store through some of the broken windows and grab a few things." Kya pats Carrie's backpack.

"Thanks." I step around the girls.

"It's a suicide mission," Carrie says.

I stop and turn with a nod. "I'm sure it is, but I have to try. I'm not prepared for winter, and I need something more than this thing to defend myself with." I wave my spiked head in the air.

"Well, good luck," Carrie says.

"You, too. Maybe we will run into each other again someday." I start away from them, aware that I am leaving behind the only humans I have seen since this shitshow began.

I gulp down the need to turn and remain with the girls heading toward the horde I already ran from, but I can't. I have to find supplies, otherwise I will not last when the snow begins to fly.

Chapter 4

T HEY WEREN'T KIDDING.

I've been scoping out the mall from the woods for the last hour but the milling of zombies in the parking lot has me chilled more than the direct wind in my face. The broken glass of the sporting goods store beckons, but it seems like the dead are concentrated there. As if they know there are things that will be used against them inside.

It's frightening.

In the distance, a siren blares and I nearly fall out of the tree I'm perched in. It's far enough away so I cannot see who triggered it, but it draws the horde. Slowly at first, but then they are all lumbering in the direction of the siren.

I glance around and slip down to the ground. It's at least the length of a football field or two between the tree line and the store. I take one more scan of my path and the surrounding area.

The zombies have lumbered twice the distance and the sound still fills the air. The minute that dies, I'm fair game.

I have no idea how long it will continue. But this is my window. With my heart clanging in my chest, I sprint across the parking lot with my stick at the ready. I don't stop when I reach the hole. I'm inside, surrounded by the dark before I realize it. I slow to a stop and blink, getting my bearings and listening for any movement over the sound of the distant alarm.

There are a few backpacks still hanging on the rack right next to me. I grab one, noting how similar it is to the ones the girls had on. I scan the store. Although there are two floors to the place, I am not too keen on making my way to the top floor where the weapons are. This floor will have to be enough and luckily, I am on the level where the shoes are and some hunting clothes.

With the efficiency of terror, I grab things that I think will fit and stuff them all into the backpack. In the nearest corner, I find camping supplies and grab a second backpack, filling it with as many adventure meals as it will hold.

On my way out, I grab a pair of hiking boots and I'm out the window and halfway to the woods when the alarm suddenly ceases. I didn't try to find cleats and right now, my primary objective is getting to safety with my backpacks intact.

My footfalls echo now that silence has fallen over the blacktop. I don't dare look. I need the tree cover and the knotted pine that I found refuge in before the siren launched the masses toward it.

My breath wheezes and the packs on my shoulders bang my back with bruising slaps, but I cannot slow down. I can hear the footfalls in the distance. The ground shakes with their speedy steps, but I clear the fence lining the woods in one side vault and scramble up the tree that afforded me safety and a view before. I flatten out on the thick branch with my legs wrapped around the trunk behind me, and balance the packs on my back. I hold my breath as a mass of zombies pass right by the fence I just jumped like a wave of destruction.

My mouth is so dry that breathing makes me need to cough, but I bite down on the back of my hand to stop it. At least the wind is still on my face and hasn't turned. Otherwise, I would be stuck in the tree for however long these beasts would be wandering about underneath me.

On the far side of the mall, another siren goes off. It's as if someone is coordinating efforts to gain entry to get things they need. I wish I had time to navigate the upstairs of the sporting goods store. At least there I could get some decent weapons. I glance at the spiked doll head that crosses over the branch in front of me, hating it, but thankful I have something long enough to strike without putting myself in immediate danger.

The masses of dead turn toward the sound and scramble across the tar in a dead run. They've become faster than I remember. When they disappear around the building, I slip down from my tree. Before I turn away from the mall, I see them. My eyebrows rise at the three men running across the lot from the direction of the first siren.

Other people *do* exist. My heart jumps in my chest, and I start to navigate the woods surrounding the mall instead of heading away from the danger. Those men staged that siren to see whether the horde would leave.

I wonder whether they saw me at all or whether they were too busy setting up the next disruption. I slow down as the siren cuts, and instead of continuing on, I find a suitable tree to climb that will keep me high enough off the ground to not get attacked. If it affords me a view, all the better.

This one isn't as easy to climb as the last, but by the time I get up to the thick branch, I have a view. A view that leaves my heart clamoring against my ribs and my stomach roiling.

The masses surged around the mall. But instead of coming my way, they collected around the opening, waiting. I shiver when the three men appear in the opening. They had raided the gun cabinets, but bullets won't help them now. They'll only draw more and more of the dead things.

Even if they had a hundred-round tommy gun, they would run out of ammunition before they wiped out the herd.

The first semi-automatic shot echoes on the air. Followed by a dozen more before the first zombie gets through the firing line.

Didn't these idiots know that you always aim for the head?

They were shooting point-blank at the zombie's chests. Perhaps they were shitty shots, I don't know, but their plan fails and before long, the gunshots stop, along with the screams.

I cry for their needless deaths as a shiver encompasses me. That could have been me. I check myself, sniffling and wiping the tears from my face before I slide down to the ground as quietly as I can. With both backpacks secure and my hellraiser staff in hand, I move away from the mall as quickly as one can go without noise.

The area on this side of the fence is not inundated with the dead, and I am thankful for the absence of rotting flesh.

As soon as I hit the end of the woods, I understand why this area is barren. No one in their right mind would cross through an endless cemetery, but that is what I am considering. I glance at the head on my stick. I haven't been in my right mind since I saw the first of the dead on that first day.

Before I head into the unknown, I sit down with my back to a tree trunk and take stock in the contents of my backpacks. I choose the food stock first, inspecting what I had just thrown into the pack. I had at least twenty meals and a few extras. The most impressive thing that I had was a water filtration tube. Unfortunately, I only swiped two water packets, so I would have to find a water source before I could eat more than two meals.

I scan the graveyard and then glance at my stock again. The food section in the store hadn't been picked over. If those girls had actually raided the store, they obviously did not know about freeze-dried food. Or if they did, then they hadn't had the time to raid the food shelves before bugging out.

At least I'll be well fed, until I freeze to death.

With that in mind, I unzip the other bag and pull out everything I hastily stuffed inside, including a pair of track sneakers that aren't too bad a fit. I could work with them. But the boots were perfect and snug, and the tag says they are waterproof, so I hit the jackpot with these. My well-worn sneakers start the pile of things that are no longer useful to me. A small part of me cringes at the idea of littering, but there is no way I am carting those things around with me, especially considering they are effectively useless now.

Besides, no one in the cemetery would mind.

I strip off my old worn sweatpants and slip into the thermal hunting pants I grabbed. My makeshift weapon holder comes off next, along with my ratty T-shirt. The new undershirt is soft on my skin, and I take a few moments to run my fingers over the ribbing. It seems to calm me even more than taking stock of what I have.

My stomach grumbles, so I put on the jacket and then stare at my weapon holder and the backpacks. The one I stuffed with food has some really neat attachments that I didn't notice until this moment. A can opener. A pocketknife and a couple webbed sides that can be used for water bottles. I bite my lip, looking between my weapon holder and the pack. I can't have both on me. The backpack seems more practical, but I need a reliable place to stash my pole and my knife without being inhibited from getting them out fast. The webbing will work to hold the knife sheath without issue. But there really is no place for my pole where I can safely stash it and retrieve it like I can with the holder I have now. But I can always use it as a weird walking stick. It's something I do not want to ditch. Not with the reach it has versus the knife, which requires hand-to-hand combat to use.

With my knife secured on the side of the backpack, I repack the food and set out a meal, along with the tin that came with the meal pack and one of the few water packets that was included in my stash. My mouth waters as I mix the powdery meal with water.

The first bite makes my jaw lock painfully and I close my eyes, working through that bite before I take a second. This one I relish. The oatmeal breakfast tastes like a five-star feast. I eat the entire thing in one sitting, tempering the need to suck it down with the need to savor the peaches and cream flavor on my tongue.

It is the sweetest meal I think I've ever had, and I actually lick the tin clean before I stow it away in my backpack. With a full belly, I stand and secure the backpack, pick up my hellraiser, and start down the small slope into the graveyard.

Chapter 5

ALL OF OUR decisions are ruled by logic and luck. Well, there's also emotion, but that always screws the pooch when acting out of emotion. The absence of the dead in this graveyard is as deceptive as the cleared parking lot of the mall when the alarm was blaring. As the hill gives way to the lines of tall gravestones, my skin crawls as the grand statues engulf me.

I slow my stroll down to a step-stop-listen-step-again framework. The food in my belly weighs heavy, like the tension in my body is ready to force it all out of my queasy stomach. I have a moment to wonder whether maybe the food was there because it had gone past its good-by date, but then I scoff. Freeze-dried food like these packs lasts years.

I focus back on my surroundings and my mind wanders back to pictures I once saw of a cemetery in the South somewhere that had wall-to-wall monuments, where horrific voodoo rites of sacrifice were portrayed. The memory chills me, along with the shadows growing long across the landscape.

I do not want to be in this garden of tombstones when night falls.

I glance at the nearest gravestone in the form of an angel statue and my eyes are pulled to the date. This poor soul has been in the ground for nearly a century, which is surprising based on how pristine the statue is. I reach out and touch it, expecting the feel of rough concrete under my fingers.

Instead, I find the smoothness of cool marble.

With every step, I'm gripping my staff tighter. Shadows slink out of nowhere, making me spin to the side of the closest statue. My heart slams in my chest and I wait with my hellraiser gripped so tight that my hands become numb.

Stop freaking out!

Even my thought-voice shook, and I nearly burst out laughing at my skittishness. If the dead were here in this cemetery, I would have already been their main course.

"It's just a cemetery," I whisper, shaking off the itch of nerves tickling my skin, and step back into the lane between mausoleums in search of an exit. What I find is quite unexpected. A fence cut the cemetery in half, which explains the total absence of zombies.

The layers of statues and crypts blocked the view of the fencing from the woods. If I had known, I would have attempted to go back the way I came. At least those milling about on the other side had not caught my scent. I slid back a couple of rows and took in the entirety of the black iron-spiked pickets enclosing this temporary safe space. I need to find a different way around because I won't have a prayer of escape if they pick up my scent.

I need a place to hunker down for the night, and I glance up at the woods in the distance. Wind filters through my hair and I choke on a breath as it hits my face. The wind is coming from the woods. I slide behind a building, away from the rumbling herd.

I can't see them, but I can hear them banging on the iron.

Damn it. I glance at the rows of mausoleums, looking for a place to hide that doesn't have any recent dead inside. At least in the confines of a crypt, I'll be masked by the stale scent of death. I finally find what I am looking for with doors that open outward. That's one thing I did note: although the masses were getting smarter and hunting in packs, they still didn't know how to pull open a door. Of course, they seem to understand pushing like they were now doing with the fence, and eventually with enough bodies, they break barriers, but I had time to evade them.

I pull the doors, and nothing happens. I blink and search for a reason they won't open. No chain exists on the handles. The handles themselves turn, but the doors don't budge.

I yank harder and the creak from behind me nearly does me in. My hands become too slick to get a grip on the handle, and I glance over my shoulder. The spikes lean too far in my direction.

If I can't get this open, I need to run for the woods and the safety of the trees. My heart hammers and I pull with everything I have. But the door only moves less than an inch. Not nearly wide enough for me to squeeze through and certainly if it's this hard to open, it will be impossible to close before they breach the opening.

With my pulse near heart attack levels, I break out in a run down the clear path between mausoleums. All this does is serve to increase the dead's velocity and ferocity on getting through the barrier.

I turn on an adjacent path, one that leads away from the crypts and into the field of statues and tombstones. I can barely see the woods in the distance. The distinct scream of metal crashing fills the air behind me, along with the heavy footfalls of a mob.

The closer I get to the end of the gravestones, the more my eyes deceive me. The trees are moving. I skid to a halt at the sight of more zombies pouring through the woods, onto the hill lining the cemetery. Without missing a step, I break a hard right, toward where I think the mall stands. Zombies are now coming from both my right and my left, and all I can see in front of me is another row of crypts.

This is not where I want to die. This cannot be my last stand. Forgotten, in a cemetery of all places.

I reach the biggest building and turn, unsheathing my knife

and wielding my hellraiser. I scream a war cry at the mounting force of zombies surrounding me, and they pause, as if they have never seen the sight of a human warrior's last stand.

I swing my hellraiser and connect with flesh. I slash out with my blade in the opposite direction, but it doesn't stop the horde. My adrenaline is set to high octane, high enough that I don't feel the first bite, or the next, or the next. I just keep lashing out like a madwoman.

Twenty, thirty zombies fall under my crushing blows before my hellraiser snaps. But I'm still standing, still screaming like a banshee as I swing my knife like a deadly pendulum.

The tax on my heart is too great and I finally succumb to the brunt of their attack.

Blood runs red from wounds that will never heal but the pain that should resonate through every fiber never reaches my brain. It's as if my nerves shut off with the overload of adrenaline.

The sunset is glorious over the cemetery. Pinks and purples, and yellows and blues paint the sky, all shadowed by a reddish hue. But then everything turns into a dull gray before it fades away.

Dumb luck finally ran out.

The End

If you enjoyed Battleground,

please consider leaving a review!

About J.E. Taylor

J.E. Taylor is a USA Today bestselling author, a publisher, an editor, a manuscript formatter, a mother, a wife, a business analyst, and a Supernatural fangirl. Not necessarily in that order. She first sat down to seriously write in February of 2007 after her daughter asked:

"Mom, if you could do anything, what would you do?"

From that moment on, she hasn't looked back.

Besides being co-owner of Novel Concept Publishing, Ms. Taylor also moonlights as a Senior Editor of Allegory E-zine, an online venue for Science Fiction, Fantasy and Horror, and co-host of the popular YouTube talk show Spilling Ink.

She lives in New Hampshire with her husband and during the summer months enjoys her weekends on the shore in southern Maine.

Visit her at www.jetaylor75.com to check out her other titles.

If you enjoyed Battleground,
check out some of J.E. Taylor's
other horror and suspense titles:

THE STEVE WILLIAMS SERIES

Special Agent Steve Williams
excels at his job, catching the
most heinous of monsters
walking the earth.

Serial killers.

When his job brings him face to face with a psychic, he struggles to accept her gifts in his neat little black and white world. Armed with her visions, along with his skills as an FBI agent, he hunts the worst of the worst, but will he catch the killer before they set their sights on him?

Unstoppable, breath stealing, and terrifying all at once.

Gripping, rich and magnificent!

The Steve Williams Series mixes compelling crime thrillers with supernatural forces that will grip the reader from page one. This six-book series takes you through some of Steve Williams' darkest cases in his FBI career.

The STEVE WILLIAMS SERIES includes Dark Reckoning, Vengeance, Hunting Season, Georgia Reign, Crystal Illusions, and Saving Face.

RUNNING FROM THE DEVIL TRILOGY

An escaped demon and a snarky cat face off against the seven deadly sins.

Escaping from Hell was just the beginning of Phoebe's problems. In Hell, she had a position of legend. A marquis of torture. But on the human plane, she is just another New York City destitute.

Before she has a chance to get her bearings on the unforgiving streets, Fate steps in and offers her a chance at redemption, but it doesn't come cheap.

She must bring in the demons that escaped alongside her while making sure no humans are harmed in the process. In order to do that, she needs to learn to live in the human world with the help of another one of Fate's parolees, a snarky cat named Smoke.

If it means never seeing the halls of Hell again, Phoebe will do anything, even battle the seven deadly sins single-handed.

SEASON OF THE DRAGON

Monsters, trust issues, betrayal, and a near death experience.

What else could go wrong?

The end of life as we knew it didn't come with a nuclear blast. It didn't come with the deadly impact of a hurdling asteroid. No. It came in a wave of illness that swept the world with fear, and in our quarantined silence, the monsters awoke.

Leviathans, serpent kings, and dragons came forth from the bowels of the Earth. The season of the dragon began with fire and fury and ended with a new world order. One in which these giant terrorists held all the power.

When Mikhail St. Clare betrays the monsters by saving me from death at their claws, I cannot trust the last remaining dragon shifter. Not when humankinds' survival is at stake, and he had a hand in our near extinction.

The only thing we seem to agree on is our desire to annihilate the leviathans and unseat the Serpent King. Our personal futures depend on ridding the earth of these murderous overlords.

We thought crossing the leviathan-patrolled city where every corner hides a hideous death was our most lethal hurdle. But building a bomb large enough to wipe out an entire species carries its own insane levels of danger.

One wrong move and we could destroy everyone living in New York instead.

Find these titles and other
fantasy and suspense titles on
J.E. Taylor's website!

www.JETaylor75.com